THE GLORY OF LOVE

Also by Jackie North

THE GLORY OF LOVE

JACKIE NORTH

The Glory of Love
Copyright © 2019 Jackie North
Published December 28, 2019

For permission requests, write to the author at jackie@jackienorth.com

This is a work of fiction. Names, characters, places, and incidents are a product of the author's imagination or are used fictitiously. Any resemblance to people, places, or things is completely coincidental.

Cover Design by Jackie North

The Glory of Love/Jackie North

ISBN:

Mobi - 978-1-942809-24-1

Print - 978-1-942809-31-9

Library of Congress Control Number: TBD

For all those who know that love is love…

And for those who know what love can be found in the most unlikely of places.

"I will always love you. I will never leave you alone."

~~ Peter Cetera
Glory of Love

Chapter One

Up on the north end of Harlin, right along Main Street, is a pool hall called The Breakers. Which is, I'll admit, not very original, nor is the place very swank. But it's decent, the floor is in one piece, the beer is cold, the floor gets swept. There's a bar in the front, and a collection of nearly-new pool tables in the back.

The owner is LGBT friendly. He's so friendly, he doesn't really give a crap what you are, as long as you pay your tab, don't break a chair over anybody's head, and respond to last call like a golden retriever on steroids. That is, right away and cheerfully.

Nobody really ever wants to leave The Breakers once it gets hopping, and I'd been a semi-regular ever since I discovered it the previous summer. It was there I'd met and fell in love with my beloved Charlie, who, in retrospect, was just a hometown boy who'd come off the sheep farm to do some experimenting.

By experimenting, I mean gay sex, and with whom, I mean me. It had been a good two months, him and me together, starting with the Fourth of July, and sex in the bathroom before the fireworks went off. We exchanged blow jobs, both of us with our cut-off shorts to our knees, me with my ass pressed against the metal door of the stall.

He had a nice body, sort of stocky and strong, and a farmer's tan that made his torso a blinding white, with that little line across his thighs which was just as long as his cock after I'd sucked him off. Our relationship had been hot like summer's fire, all flames and sparks when we got together, and then drowsy, flickering soft when we'd fall asleep together.

Charlie had sweet brown eyes, and a head full of mink brown hair, and this, along with his sleepy smile and his amazing thighs, made me pretty hot for him. Long about Labor Day, I was falling for him hard, and wanting more time with him than I was getting. I'm a little selfish like that.

I see what I want and go after it. Sure I could have been a lawyer, but that was too much time in an office, too much shirt-and-tie for me. I liked being Tier 1 support at the software company I worked for just fine. Tier 1 guys and gals got the tough questions, rather than Tier 3 folks, who usually had to solve the "try and turn it off and then on again and see if it works" questions.

But come September, Charlie was off to CSU in Ft. Collins to get his animal husbandry degree. Leaving me high and dry with my cock unsucked and my body feeling the ghost of his touch, my soul empty, like I'd been drained dry and would end up ugly and old and alone.

Hey, give me a break! I can be alone, I'm not that kind of guy who needs someone all the time in my life. But being with Charlie, who'd been introduced to me at The Breakers and who, it seemed, warmed to me right away, was awesome from the start.

He was funny and sweet, laughed a lot, and knew something about software to understand what I did for a living. I hadn't the faintest idea about sheep, but was willing to learn. That was how we started, with the very American question "What do you do for a living?" as if what you did to earn money was what defined you.

What I did didn't define me, though I enjoyed the hell out of it, solving puzzles and saving folks from their own stupidity on the internet. Like Aunt Edna from Manhattan, Kansas. She'd been one of my first rescues, as she'd actually clicked on the link in the email she'd gotten, and now her computer was acting funny.

Well, I'd saved her and taught her about what not to do with those too-good-to-be-true emails she sometimes got, and she would only talk to me when she called in. A lot of my regular customers were like that, and so I got a cube by the window, and access to the good coffee machine on the 7th floor. I was in heaven. My bosses loved me.

Anyway, enough about my job. It's what I do, not who I am, and most of my friends are in the software industry, too. We run together, and we curse together, and we laugh together. One is into Legos, another is into Star Wars, still another swears by WOW. Me? I like hooking up, and The Breakers is one of my favorite places to do that.

I like the feel of another man's cock in my hand. I like to whisper in his ear when I make him come, and I like the blissful after-time, when we're just together in the sheets, this imaginary guy and I. Where he tells me funny stories, and I laugh, and we drink coffee together, and then go back to dozing.

I might even say, though you have to promise not to tell anyone, that the reason I cruise and am willing to have sex at the drop of a hat is for that after-time. Where I don't have to be anyone, or help anyone, I can just be there, in that dozy, sleepy, relaxed moment.

Okay, I did admit all of this to one guy at work, Laurie, but he went on vacation to Wyoming and never came back. I already had feelings about Wyoming and not good ones, not after Mathew Sheppard.

You couldn't get me to cross the boundary between Colorado and Wyoming, not for all the money in the world. And when Laurie didn't come back and some of us, including me, got questioned by the po-po, my efforts not to go into Wyoming became a rock solid thing. Didn't want anything to do with the state. No way, no how.

So then I have this friend by the name of Troy. (My name is Nick, by the way.) Now, Troy's a party guy, like I am, and he'll sleep with anyone or anything. He likes getting it up the ass, and there's nothing wrong with that, right? But he's a jerk about it, and will share details to even the most unwilling of audiences, who prefer not to know the graphic nitty gritty about prep and aftercare.

Maybe those folks are like me, and they have this romantic idea of cuddling in the sheets after a good session of sexy fun times, and don't want to know. I don't always want to know, but sometimes with Troy, his mouth is open and the words are coming out and just wow. Shut up, Troy. I went to college with him, we roomed sometimes, and now I'm kind of stuck with him as a friend. We have a history, see.

At any rate, I'd been missing Charlie and it was coming up to New Year's. Hey, no comments, okay? Yes, I was moping and missing him because we'd had those mornings, him and I. Those coffee-in-bed kind of mornings. And his mouth was fabulous. Sure I'd had to put up with him talking about sheep, and making sheep jokes, but it had been worth it, I thought.

Back to New Year's. It was a few days before when the phone rang. I picked it up, feeling bored, and lonely and sorry for myself, and answered even though it was Troy.

"Hey, bro," said Troy, trying to be cool, like he does. "New Year's Eve is coming."

"Every year," I said dryly. "Can't hardly stop it." Sorry, but I can't help but be a little cruel to Troy. It doesn't reflect well on me, but he just invites it, you know?

"The Breaker's is having a glory hole in the basement again this year."

"Didn't we all almost get thrown out, we got so rowdy?"

That party had been a blast, but it had gotten wild towards the end. Jonas, the owner, had been on the verge of calling the cops, though how he would have managed to explain the row of glory holes in his basement might have made the evening more exciting than he would have cared for.

"I don't know," I said slowly, and this time it wasn't just to irritate Troy, but because I really couldn't feel myself pulling my cock out and sticking it in a hole for a stranger to suck on. God, I'm such a softie if I really actually need to see the other guy's face, and enjoy the moment with them rather than being distanced by a piece of cardboard or whatever Jonas was going to put up this year.

Last year, the wall had been made of plywood, with a layer of black cloth over the ceiling to make it look like nighttime, even though it was already pretty dark in that basement of his. The inside of each little cubby had been decorated like a Christmas tree, and the lick of moisture on my dick had reflected the glints of tinsel and green and blue and red lights. But it had been empty, an empty pleasure and a lackluster evening all the way around.

I had left, I'll have you know, before the real rowdy

crowd had shown up, but I'd heard about it. Troy had stayed, of course, but he's like that.

"Please?" asked Troy, and his voice was all pathetic, like he knows I can't resist. "I'll buy you your first two rounds, okay? Say you'll go."

"Okay." There, it was done. I was going to be out on New Year's Eve, and I would probably, no, make that most definitely, get my dick sucked. That would make it worth leaving the house for. Right?

Wanting to look my best, I thought about getting my groom on, doing all those things that would make me nice to be near. Now, I'm already nice to be near, to hear the way Charlie told it. That I was good to be near, that I had strong arms, that I had nice abs, that he liked the way I was trimmed. He once told me my smile had sharp teeth, like an animal. Another time that my eyes were emerald green, my hair as black as ink. But then, he'd been drinking, so I didn't put much stock in it.

And it wasn't that I couldn't be bothered. While I like giving head as much as receiving it, I just didn't want some nameless, faceless encounter that might or might not be reciprocal.

Some guys like to be used, and I'm not against that, but I like to really know, by the expressions on their faces, that they really, really get off on it. But the day of the glory hole shindig, I worked out, showered and shaved, took some gel to my hair and threw on my favorite soft shirt, the thinnest chambray I'd picked up at the thrift store because some bozo had torn the hem.

Well, as I tucked the hem into my jeans and tightened the belt, nobody would notice. We weren't going to be undressing each other, unless it was with our eyes in the dimly lit cellar of The Breakers. We were going to be sucking dick, and for that we could leave our clothes on. Not sure why that made me feel glum as I locked up my apartment and went out to my old beater to warm up the engine, but it did.

Chapter Two

Traffic in Harlin is always a surprise to me, but it shouldn't be. We have an active and old fashioned downtown, a place where people drive to to go to the post office or the courthouse or the library. Seeing as it was New Year's Eve, it was even busier than usual, so I just took my time and drove slowly up Main Street to the intersection at the north end of town where The Breaker's was.

I parked as far out in the empty lot behind the bar as I could to make it easier to leave whenever I wanted to. Then I strode across the parking lot, blowing smoke rings of frost in front of me as I went. My jacket was an old Carhartt I found for five bucks, yes, at the thrift store again, but it was thick and warm and what I'd not spent on it was tucked away in savings.

Okay, yes, I'll admit it, I'm one of those guys, okay? I have nice clothes, fashionable thin shoes and all the rest of it, but I don't spend spend spend, even though I could. I want to move out of my apartment one day and buy a little place where I can walk around naked without worrying about the neighbors seeing in.

All my pals at the software company are busy spending their pay, their bonuses, but not me. Just don't tell anyone, right? I never have, not even Charlie. It's how my dad taught me and even though he's not around anymore, I still listen to his advice.

I strutted a bit as I entered the warm atmosphere of The Breakers, feeling all eyes upon me, but pretending not to give a damn. By the set of my shoulders, they all knew why I was there, wearing my easy-to-unzip blue jeans for the very purpose of pulling my dick out and closing my eyes as the sense of pleasure rushed through me.

There were some folks just sitting on bar stools buying their cheap beer so they could watch to see who went into the basement and how long it took them to come out. Other guys were standing by the door to the basement, their hands in their pockets, like they were feeling for dollar bills that they would hand over to the broad-shouldered bouncer who stood waiting to let people in or out.

Jonas had it arranged so that only fifteen guys would be downstairs at a time. Why that number? There were five glory holes, each one a little private room, swags of cloth and the darkness making it impossible to see how each couple got on, or who had paired up with whom. The other five could wait their turn, and give off the kind of nervous tension that made it all very exciting, pulsing with energy, the smell of salt and sex.

Last year there had been a kind of thrumming music in the background and I hadn't been able to figure out if it was just zen instrumental, or if it was actually Evanescence without words. Jonas had also piped in some scent, I swear, which was either vanilla, or that Mountain Lodge candle everyone's always talking about. The combination of all of this told me that Jonas should have charged more than twenty bucks for half an hour, but I suspect he knew that.

The Breakers was a hopping bar with or without the New Year's glory hole setup.

"Hey," someone said from behind me and I knew it was Troy even before I felt the clamp of his hand on my shoulder.

"Yeah," I said as I turned and brushed his hand off, but gently. The guy can't really help it that his skin always feels clammy to me. "I'm here. Where's my beer."

Troy had my beer in his hands, a green bottle of ice cold Stella, and I took it with a nod of thanks. Just because he's the kind of guy who will lick your boots for nothing doesn't mean he deserves to have abuse heaped on his head, but I always did wish he'd grow a little backbone.

"You paid yet?" I asked him.

"First one here," said Troy, with his nervous laugh. "First one in the door."

"Jonas appreciates your patronage for sure," I said, remembering too late that the blank look on Troy's face wasn't for effect, he honestly didn't know what the word *patronage* meant. Nor would he care to look it up later and learn something. "You're a good customer, Troy," I added, more gently. Then I sucked back some beer and sighed, wincing as the hops hit my throat.

"My cousin is here," he said to me, poking me with his elbow, like he was sharing a huge secret. "I brought him to get him out of the house for one night."

"Yeah?" I asked not really interested, as I could only imagine a carbon copy of Troy. Maybe the cousin would be a little shorter or wider or whatever, but with those same puppy dog eyes and mouse-brown hair. The narrow shoulders that he stooped forward, trying to hide his height and lack of muscle.

"Up from Denver," said Troy. "He came out to his folks

and they shipped him to his aunt and uncle, which are my aunt and uncle."

"The religious ones?" I asked with a shudder. I'd never met them, maybe waved at them from the sidewalk in front of their house one time, but they were Christians. Not Catholics but something else, Methodists or something.

"Yeah," said Troy with a shrug, which I took to mean that he didn't give a damn about how his poor cousin was suffering under their roof, but that was Troy for you. Plus, it said something about the cousin that he was willing to stay with people his parents had shipped him to because they didn't like the fact that he was gay.

"Right over there," said Troy, pointing, as though I'd asked to be introduced. "His name is Daniel."

"Oh, yeah?" I wasn't interested, I really, really wasn't, but then again, I felt a little sorry for Troy, even though I shouldn't be. He had plenty of friends, but always seemed oblivious to whatever I was going through. Which, right now, was the realization that I'd probably made a huge mistake coming out tonight, and that I probably wasn't going to shell out the twenty bucks to go to the room where the glory holes were.

"Right over there," said Troy, pointing even harder now, like I was supposed to do something about it.

Squinting through the crowd at the bar, I tried to figure out which was the cousin and which were the folks standing in my way so I could get this over with.

"Here," said Troy. "I'll help you."

He dragged me up to the bar, clutching on the sleeve of my jacket as he pulled me through the crowd, acting like he was my rescuer from a life of loneliness. As long as he didn't start talking about the various viscosities of anal lube, I figured I could get through the next five minutes of awkwardness meeting someone I didn't really want to meet.

When we got close, Troy shoved his way right up to the bar, taking me with him, and then slapped his hand on the bar in front of someone who was just receiving their drink. Which I noticed, with a slight bit of derision, was a lemon drop martini. Nothing wrong with the drink, mind you, but this wasn't that kind of bar, and Jonas' wait staff probably didn't understand the nuances of a freshly shaved curl of lemon peel in the bottom of the glass.

I was looking at the glass and thinking there was way too much sugar on that rim, and that the food coloring was way too yellow, when I realized someone was looking at me.

"This is Daniel," said Troy, giving me a shove so that I'd pay attention to exactly what Troy wanted me to and not anything else. One of his more annoying traits. "Daniel, this is my friend, Nick."

"Hello," said Daniel, in a voice that was almost too quiet to hear over the babble and din. "It's nice to meet a friend of Troy's."

Of course any friend of Troy's was probably way into anal sex and graphic oversharing, but then, this Daniel fellow probably knew that. I wondered how much of the conversation about me, where Troy had told Daniel about me, had actually been about me and how much had been about anal sex and aftercare.

"Nice to meet you," I said in return, and then I sort of blinked at him. He was too well-groomed to be the kind of guy to hang out at a place like The Breakers, like he'd come fresh from a corporate meeting, all dapper, his hair gleaming golden in the dim overhead lights. Then I wondered, on the heels of that, why a guy as pretty as he was would need to spend twenty bucks for the privilege of going down to the basement.

"You here for the glory holes?" I asked him, just to get it out in the open.

He took a quick breath, his eyes going a little wide. As he shifted his body, he stepped more into the little circle of light that I was standing in, and I was able to get a good long look. His cheeks were flushed, and his eyes so very blue in comparison. He had one of those rich boy haircuts, parted on the side, with his forelock hanging over one smoky eyebrow.

I couldn't figure out, just then, if he realized how good looking he was, or if everything handsome thing about him, from his golden hair to his broad shoulders to his trim waist, was a happy, gorgeous accident. Probably not an accident. He probably was full of ego to go with this little display of emo I was now witnessing.

"I was," he said, almost stammering but, with a shake of his head, he seemed to catch himself. "Now, I don't know. I think it would be too much for my first time."

"Your first time?" I waved my bottle of beer at him, laughing with my mouth open. "So we've got a virgin in our midst?"

Troy laughed like a drain. The bartender was smirking, too, but Daniel, he kept his cool and his glance around him was like steel. This impressed me, I can tell you that.

His cheeks were even more pink now, but he took a sip of his lemon drop martini and then held his head high as if inviting even more snickers and looks. I was about to dismiss him then and there as too proud and too beautiful for me to want to mess with when I caught a glimpse of something in his eyes. It was only there for a second and then was gone.

"Yes, if you must know," said Daniel with tart dismissal.

"His folks gave him the old heave ho when he came out to them," said Troy. "I told you that, right? He's staying with my aunt and uncle."

"The Christians," I said, not bothering to hide the derision in my voice. "Good luck with that."

"They're good people," said Daniel. I thought this maybe was by reflex, as though that's what he thought he was supposed to say. But then he laughed, and took a sip of his drink. "But my folks don't know, I guess, just how good."

"What's that?" I asked, and yeah, I even leaned forward because this was not the response I would have expected. None of this was. He was around my age, I figured, and old enough to have his own place, and yet here he was, staying with his religious relatives because his parents told him to.

"They're religious, sure," said Daniel. "But not the kind my parents thought they were."

"Oh, who cares about that," said Troy. "And who's coming with me to the glory holes? You brought your money, Nick?"

"Yeah, I brought it," I said, taking a slow sip of my beer. "Been there, done that." Which was my way of telling Troy that no, I was not coming with him, but that I didn't care if he went. But Troy being who he was, stepped close and jostled my elbow.

"You came for the glory holes last year," he said. "Why not this year? You said you would, c'mon!"

"Because I'm not, Troy," I said as calmly as I could, seeing as how his action had caused me to shake my beer. A large bubble of it was slipping out of the mouth of the bottle and down the side, yes, just like it had spent itself with pleasure.

"You're missing out," said Troy, sneering at me, like I was the lowest loser in town.

"You have fun for me," I said to him as he walked away. Then I turned back to Daniel, who was finishing off his martini like he was about to bail on the whole night and go home.

"You need a ride?" I asked him, not really sure why I was asking, but he looked like he wanted out of there.

"You don't have to feel sorry for me," he said, his mouth pulling into a frown as he wiped crumbs of sugar from his lips. "I'll decide when the time is right for me to become an ex-virgin."

"Oh yeah?" I shook my head, wanting to break away from the mesmerizing play of his fingers on his mouth, and swallowed the last of my beer, plonking the empty bottle on the counter. "With your aunt and uncle hanging over you, praying every other minute. That's got to be a lot of fun."

He surprised me by laughing, looking down his nose at me all at the same time.

"They did pray over me, as a matter of fact," he said. "And they said that since God made me, I was blessed in the sight of the Lord. The prayers were to help me make good choices tonight."

"Did they know you were coming to a glory hole party?" I asked, a bit stung by the laugh and confused by the admission.

"Not exactly," he said. "Not at all, as a matter of fact. I told them I was going to a bar, this bar, and that I'd be home after midnight."

"Where, no doubt, they will pray over you some more."

"You don't get it, do you." Daniel turned to look

around him as though he didn't want to be overheard saying what he was about to tell me. "My folks sent me to them because they think that Aunt Louise and Uncle Ralph are the kind of Christians who would try to talk me out of being gay. They never took the time to know them, so they're dead wrong."

"You could get your own place," I said, not spelling out my unnecessary opinion that he was old enough and certainly didn't need Mom and Dad taking care of him.

"And I will." Daniel took a breath and shrugged his shoulders. "I just didn't realize how hard my folks would take it. How hard I would take their rejection. Louise and Ralph offered me a place under their roof, so I took it, just till I can get a job up here, instead of in Denver."

The boy was going through some transitions, that was for certain. But he was being level-headed about it, not spinning off in a whirl of abject depression or victimhood, even though it must have hit him hard that his parents had thought that time spent with Christians would be enough to un-gay him.

"You still need that ride?" I asked him. "If Troy's staying and you want to go, I could give you a lift."

"It's not anywhere near midnight," he said, half turning away from me as he pushed his now-empty martini glass away from him. The movement was strong and quick, and then he paused as if considering getting another one, just to make the whole evening more bearable.

"Yeah, but you look like you need to get out of here," I said. "Like coming out for a visit to the glory hole was Troy's idea."

"It was. How did you know?" Then he laughed again, dipping his head down as though he was ashamed of laughing at Troy's expense. "He made it sound fun," said Daniel, looking at me, more serious now. "And I thought it would be a good way to not be a virgin anymore."

"For somebody else, maybe," I said. "Not for you."

I waited for him to get all pissed off that I dare make an observation and have an opinion about somebody I'd just met, but he didn't. He looked at me for a long minute, those blue eyes so very serious, and then he pushed his forelock off his forehead with his fingers.

It was a sexy move, like he was posing for a photo shoot in a magazine, and there were other people looking at him. I realized, all at once, that he didn't know how good he looked. That, or he didn't care. Either way, he deserved a ride home and I meant to give it to him.

"Let me get my coat," he said, then pulled it from the barstool he'd been standing next to, and shrugged it on with careless flair. "I live on the west side of town."

The west side of town was the rich side, where all the places had a view of the mountains of some kind. I lived in a small apartment on the east side of town, in one of the newer developments that had gone up without much thought to long-term livability.

He was telling me, it seemed, so I would be forewarned that he was one of those rich kids. Tell me something I didn't already know, right? His coat was soft wool, by the looks of it, and his haircut had to cost at least a hundred bucks.

Everything about him was new, but had that artfully rumpled look of having been broken in by careful wear. I especially liked the scent of his cologne, also expensive, as I followed him out of The Breakers and across the frosty air of the parking lot.

"I'm over here," I said, leading the way between the parked cars to my old Honda, still serviceable after many, many miles.

I didn't open the door for him, but I clicked the unlock button on my key fob and made sure he was in before I got in. Then I started up the engine and warmed up the car before driving slowly out of the parking lot.

The clock on my dash said it was just after 11 pm, and the traffic was as busy as if it was in the middle of the day, what with everyone dashing around trying to get to the perfect spot before it struck midnight. Me, I was taking some guy home to his religious aunt and uncle, a virgin guy who I probably wasn't even going to get to kiss.

Following his directions, I soon ended up parking along the sloping curb in front of a newish house in a nice part of town. The front door was already opened by the time we both got out of the car, and a woman with long brown hair was waving us to come closer. Beneath the porch light, she seemed nice, and I tried to recalibrate my earlier negative opinion of her with the woman who now kissed her nephew on the cheek, and turned to me with a smile.

"I'm thinking the bar wasn't as fun as you'd thought?" she asked, and though the question was for both of us in general, I knew it was aimed at Daniel. "That's a shame, truly. But you're here now. Won't you invite your friend in? We're about to have a glass of cheap champagne and watch the ball drop in Time Square."

"Uh, no thanks," I said, having visions of a lengthy prayer session at some point during the festivities. "I better get on home before the drunks come out of the bars."

The expression on her face told me a lot, not all of which I could translate into something that made sense. That folks would be drunk later, probably too drunk to drive, was of concern to her. As was, at the same time, the idea that getting that drunk was a waste of energy and time.

I looked at Daniel, and saw it in his eyes that I was free

to go. So, with a quick salute as I touched my finger to my forehead, I got back into my car and drove away. By the time I checked my rearview mirror, they had already gone inside and closed the door behind them.

As for me, I wended my lonely way homeward, my dick unsucked. Which was not a great start to the New Year.

Chapter Three

DURING JANUARY, MY JOB BECOMES AN UNBALANCED MIX OF boredom and stress. Boredom because there was a slump in sales, as there always was, and stressful because we were all trying to justify our jobs. Sure, we got more phone calls from customers who had just purchased our software over the holidays, and yes, I was glad to hear that Aunt Edna had weathered the storm in her part of the country. But it made going to work more stressful than usual.

The coffee machine on the 7th floor was doing double duty every day. By the time the first Friday in January came around, I was so wired on caffeine that I could have handed someone a spatula to scrape me off the ceiling.

Which was why I not only answered the phone call from Troy, but also agreed to meet him at The Breakers around 7 pm. That gave me enough time to get home, shower off the sweat of the day, have a quick shave, and put on a clean set of clothes that spoke less about my ability to fix software and more about my ability to get naked real fast. Yeah, I wore my chambray shirt again, on account of I liked how soft it felt on my shoulders. Nobody would notice I was wearing the same thing, at least not at The Breakers.

The gravel and dirt parking lot was crowded on a Friday night, which was normal because, even without the glory hole setup in the basement, it was a happening place. I locked my car, checked for my wallet and my keys, and pulled up the collar of my Carhartt jacket against the chill, making my way to the door in record time. Once inside, I grabbed a spot at the bar, ordered a Stella, and took a deep breath as I swallowed that first, crisp sip. And sighed. The week had gone on forever.

Looking around, I saw Troy on the far side of one of the pool tables, and he most certainly wasn't playing pool. He saw me out of the corner of his eye as he was flirting with some guy, nodded, and did not come over to the bar. Which was fine by me. Troy got on my nerves typically within the first five minutes of meeting up with him and then every other minute thereafter.

The area in front of the bar got pretty crowded, with bodies pushing a bit as they adjusted to where they were and where they wanted to be. Me, I sipped on my beer and was glad to not be at work. Would I get laid tonight, now, there was another question entirely that I wasn't sure I wanted to ask. Survey said: maybe not.

When I was about halfway through my beer, I felt a movement behind me, and maybe a light tap on my shoulder. That kind of thing happens in a crowded bar, so I didn't pay much attention until I inhaled that amazing cologne that Daniel had been wearing New Year's Eve. Then I turned, and there he was, standing quite close, on account of the conditions.

He had that same handsome air about him, the same sleek look, golden haired and blue eyed, standing out from everybody else like there'd been a spotlight aimed at him from somewhere. His attire was much more relaxed, no button down shirt this time, only a fancy t-shirt that looked like it might be made out of silk, as it slithered across his skin when he turned to chivvy into the place next to me.

"Hey," I said, giving a jerk of my chin by way of acknowledgement, the way that guys did when they wanted to be casual. Which I did, but my heart sped up a little bit in spite of my best efforts. Because, yes, I'd not gotten his phone number when I dropped him off, and he'd not asked for mine, but really, I hadn't been able to put him out of my mind and there he was.

"Hello," he said, looking away as he grabbed the barstool next to mine and gestured at the bartender in a way that was endlessly cool without even trying. "I'll have a Moscow mule please."

Right on the tip of my tongue was the joke that he'd just asked for a drink that was fancier than the bar he was drinking it in, but he just arched his smoky eyebrow at me, and so the joke was on me. I was the one who couldn't help but be affected by how stunning he was, so I motioned at the bartender to make it two Moscow mules, and then arched my eyebrow right back at him.

This made him smile and showed off his cheekbones and his dimples and that rosy pink mouth and I didn't quite know what to do with myself.

When our drinks came, his shoulders relaxed, and I heard him sigh, as though to himself.

"How are the aunt and uncle?" I asked.

"Fine," he said. "A bit sad, now that I've moved out."

"You got your own place?" I took a swallow of the Moscow mule and remembered the kick the drink had. "That was fast."

"Yes, it was," he said. "But it had to be. I'm an independent fellow, you see."

23

"Yes, I see," I said to him. "Well, here's to new apartments," I added, and we both raised our copper mugs and clinked them together. "What do you do when you're not hanging out here?"

"I'm a CPA," he said. "There's always jobs for that, so I got one in town. Makes the commute a whole lot shorter, I can tell you."

"I'm a software engineer," I said, almost hating the banality of this kind of exchange of information. And maybe he did too, as he clasped his little copper mug in both hands, and made a small shrugging motion with his shoulders.

"I came tonight looking for you," he said, focused on his drink, as though someone somewhere was forcing him to confess this.

"You did?" My voice rose on the question, though I found I was secretly pleased.

"Yes," he said, nodding at his hands. Then he straightened up, shoulders sensuous beneath his silk t-shirt, and looked at me. "You gave me a ride home when I needed a ride home. And, you didn't make a fuss about me being a virgin, too scared to get the glory hole experience I'd come for."

This was important to him, I could tell by the solemnity with which he told me. Any other guy would not have ever mentioned that he was a virgin, nor would most have admitted that they'd been scared. But not Daniel, no. He told it like it was, though the fact that he was telling it to me, well, that puffed me up with pride.

"It's not your scene," I said, doing my best to be casual. "Nothing wrong with that."

"It's yours, I think," he said, taking a sip of his drink. I liked watching him swallow and I liked the way a little bit of golden hair curled beneath his ear.

"Last year," I said, my voice coming out more harshly than I'd intended. "I was in a mood last year, and Troy talked me into it. This year, I thought I wanted to do it, but decided that no, I did not. There's nothing wrong with me changing my mind, is there?"

Before the words were even out of my mouth I realized that what I was saying, even if only to myself, was that I would let him experiment on me, if he wanted. If he needed someone to share that first kiss with, him with that rosy pink mouth and those cute dimples, sign me up. If he needed someone to give him his first blow job, my whole body was suddenly on fire with a hundred, no, make that a million, *yes, please, I'll be happy to oblige.*

Not that I could say any of this out loud. Not to a guy who I wanted to woo, not to scare off. Maybe it was just enough that he would trust me like he was. Or maybe it wasn't. Maybe I should just learn to be patient.

"So what kind of software work do you do?" he asked.

"Customer support," I said. "I take the tough calls. You know, when Aunt Edna calls up crying because she's lost all her pictures of her cats and can't find them. Although," I added, because Aunt Edna was always nice to me, "she learns more about computers every day. Is willing to learn, you know?"

I had no idea why I was going on about Aunt Edna, but he was sitting there looking at me like he was trying to figure me out.

"So you going to let me kiss you or what?" I asked, blurting out what I'd wanted say pretty much since the moment I met him. But it was the wrong thing to say. His whole body tightened up and he turned away, as if surveying the bar for someone more interesting than me. Someone nicer, more gentlemanly.

"Maybe I'll just go home," he said. He pulled his coat from his lap and slipped it on.

"Can I walk you?"

"To my car?" he asked, standing up. "I'm perfectly capable of walking to my car, you know."

"I do know." I stood up and shrugged my shoulders, and now we were both standing quite close between the bar stools. "I just want to, okay? After you."

Giving a little bow, I gestured that he should go first and then I followed him out into the parking lot. Like me, he'd parked his car, an old Toyota truck, as far away from everyone else as possible, to avoid getting the doors dinged.

"You're an accountant, and you have this beater?" I shook my head at his truck, which was at least ten years old.

"I'm a CPA, and yes," he said, unlocking it with an actual key, for crying out loud. "I save tons by not kowtowing to the latest trend in huge trucks with six wheels and four doors."

While I mouthed the word *kowtowing*, I mulled this over in my head. Here was a guy, pretty as a picture, who thought about money the same way I did. Be frugal. Buy stuff that lasts and take care of it. Enjoy life, but do it on your own scale.

All mantras that I lived by, and while Troy would have no idea what I meant by *mantra*, Daniel would. And not only that, they were his mantras, too, as far as I could tell. Now, not only was my whole body geared up to want to be with him, something inside me was already shouting with pleasure.

A smart guy stood in front of me, a handsome smart guy. And I was letting him get in his car and drive away before I got his phone number, yet again. The exhaust fumes from his truck stung the inside of my nose, and the air was cold on the back of my neck. I could go back inside, or I could go home, so I went home.

As I drove to my apartment, I realized I could ask Troy for Daniel's contact info. Or I could drive by his aunt and uncle's place and knock on their door, but that would be stalking, right? Stalking was the perfect way to scare a guy like this off, and I wanted him to come to me, not run from me.

Yes, it's the truth. I wanted to hold hands with him at the bar, and to spend Saturday night on the couch watching old movies. And, yeah, I wanted to take his cock in my mouth and suck him off, and hold his hips while he writhed beneath me. I wanted all those things, and stupid me, I didn't have a phone number.

So what did I do after that? Why, I went to The Breakers for a week straight. Every single night I was there, at the bar, drinking my Stella. I'd go home, shower and shave, make myself presentable and then head on out to the bar.

I played pool, I drank beer, I made jokes, and joined in the fun. The whole time I was watching the front door to see if it was him opening it and letting all the cold air in. From time to time I'd circle around the place, just to make sure he'd not slipped in without me noticing.

But he never showed. And I cursed myself for being an idiot.

Chapter Four

THE GOOD THING IS THAT, JUST LIKE AUNT EDNA, I CAN learn from my own mistakes, and took a break from my mini-stalking. So on Friday, instead of going yet again to The Breakers, I went past my apartment, turned north on Main Street and went to Five Guys Burgers. Which, if you don't already know, is the best burger place in the entire world, maybe the universe. I hadn't showered that morning, nor shaved, and so looked rather more like I was about to go into the woods with my axe with my frayed jeans and paint-stained work boots.

I parked and went inside, pulling a twenty out of my wallet because I already knew what I wanted. And, like a tiny miracle, there he was standing in line.

I scooted in behind him, and resisted the impulse to poke him or even touch him. I just stood there and breathed in his scent while admired the back of his sweet neck. Like me, he was dressed down for Friday, although, to be honest, he looked pretty dapper in that flannel shirt.

And his backside? I'd never seen anything so pert in blue jeans. It made my mouth water, and yeah, I wanted to run my hands all up and down him, but patience was my byword, and I knew I wanted to be in it for the long haul.

Was I in love? No way! But he was cool and distant, which just drew me closer, and jerking off each night in the shower hadn't done anything to dispel the mystery that was Daniel. I didn't even know his last name, but there I was, mooning over him like a lovesick calf.

He must have sensed me there, for after he put in his order, he turned his head and looked me right in the eye.

"I'm not stalking," I said hurriedly. "I mean I was, but you never showed at The Breakers so I gave up and came here. Not that I thought you'd be here, but—"

"You went to The Breakers to wait for me?" His eyebrows rose, and in his eyes was a look of softness, of questioning.

"Every night," I stated boldly. "Hoping you'd show. And here you are."

"Here we are," he said with a smile.

It seemed like an invitation, so after I ordered my food I took my receipt, filled my drink cup at the soda dispenser, and joined him at the table he'd picked out. It was by the windows, but right in the corner, which was where he was sitting, almost as though he didn't like people walking in back of him. Which made me feel a little bad about breathing down his neck like I had. But he was nice enough to get both our bags and he fetched straws and napkins and ketchup and malt vinegar.

We ate for a little while in silence, the way guys do, and I was getting a hardon just watching him eat. The way he licked his lips. The way he sucked on that straw. The way he swallowed. Good grief. Here I was with a porn movie in my head, having to reach down to adjust the crotch of my jeans, and there he was just innocently eating his fries.

When he was halfway through his cheeseburger, he

wiped his hands on his napkin and looked at me. Then he sighed, long and slow, like he was resigned to sitting with me and wasn't enjoying it very much.

"Why are you still a virgin?" I asked him.

And, at the same time, he asked me, "Why were you waiting at the bar for me?"

A little silence fell, broken only by the quick, shouted orders from the grill, the sound of the soda machine going, and the ubiquitous rock n' roll that constantly played at Five Guys.

"Flip you to see who answers first," I said, laughing as I chomped on some fries.

"I asked Troy about you," said Daniel, though I was more interested in the way his tongue curled at the corner of his mouth, like he was tasting the words.

"You asked around about little old me?" I put my hand to my heart in mock-surprise.

"No, I only asked Troy," he said. His eyebrows drew together like he was trying to be serious, but I could see the response to my joke in his eyes. This guy had a sense of humor, all right, though it might be a little buried at the moment. "Just Troy."

"And?"

"Troy doesn't understand you," said Daniel, slowly, as though carefully picking his way through what he wanted to say.

"Ain't that the truth." I nodded, but didn't add half the dumb-shit things Troy had gotten himself caught up in. "But he's not a bad guy, all things considered."

"Aunt Louise and Uncle Ralph are praying for him, they told me."

This made me laugh for some reason, as prayers weren't what Troy needed. More, he needed a guiding hand and maybe a gentle smack upside his head to keep

31

him out of the wrong bedroom. Daniel's response was a quiet chuckle as he dipped his chin and then looked up at me through those incredibly long eyelashes of his, which made my heart skip several beats.

"I wouldn't want to be your experiment," he said. "Like Charlie was your experiment."

"Oh no, shit no." I almost slammed the table as I said this, but stopped the palm of my hand from hitting the table just in time. "Troy's got it all wrong. It was the other way around. Charlie experimented on me because he wasn't sure. Now he is sure, and off he went. To animal school."

"To be a vet," said Daniel. And while he hadn't said anything about Troy being wrong, I could tell he believed me that Troy had made a mistake.

"Yes, that's right."

Part of me wanted to start explaining all of the things I was feeling, but the other part of me, sober and smart even in the dead of night, knew that I should wait and hear him out.

"About me being a virgin this long," said Daniel. "I know you want to know."

He looked around Five Guys, but really, we were at a table at the far end of the restaurant, and though it was chilly by the windows, it was a pretty private spot. The street lights were starting to come on, shining through the glass in speckles of silver and gold.

"Yes, about that."

"I wasn't sure," said Daniel. "I came through high school in a blissful haze of unawareness. I had inklings, and thoughts, but I didn't connect them to myself, to how I felt about men. But in college I knew, started to know, anyway. Then, when I came out to my parents at Christmas—"

"Always a good time," I said sarcastically.

"—and they were very angry, it made me realize that yes, I felt that way, and how dare they—"

Here Daniel stopped, his face going flushed as he swallowed hard. It was then I knew that his parents' rejection had affected him more than he'd let on, right up to that very moment.

There was passion and fire under that cool exterior but, while I still wanted to get into his jeans, I wanted to touch that fire and hold it in my two hands. Nestle it close and keep it glowing. Which is not, you have to understand, how I had ever felt about anyone else in my life. Ever.

In the past, I could spin my web and score a night in bed with some delicious fellow. Of late, that way of going about things had become rather stale. But with Daniel, I had a feeling it would never grow stale, and I would never tire of seeing the flash and spark in his eyes, never tire of the way his hands, those elegant fingers handled a burger and fries like he was eating caviar on toast tips and washing it down with fine brandy.

And, even more, I adored the way he looked at me then, asking without words for me to understand. Though why me, I didn't quite know yet. But I wanted to.

"That's a shitty thing," I said. "It's good to be honest with your folks, and then, at least, you know the truth, right? Better to know up front, then you can make good decisions. Still, it's shitty, and there's no denying that."

He cocked his head to the side, his eyes appraising me like he was seeing me there for the first time.

"That's very profound," he said.

"Not what you expected from a guy in the software business?"

"Not what I'd expect from someone of Troy's acquaintance," he replied.

"College roommates," I said, lifting both of my hands, palms out, as if asking for leniency. "Don't ask."

"I don't have to," he said, smiling again as he took a suck on his straw. "Unfortunately I can imagine it quite well."

We finished our meal in a companionable silence, and I thought about getting a chocolate shake that we could share like Lady and the Tramp, but decided against it. If our lips were going to meet, or if we were going to stare into each others' eyes, I wanted it to be in private.

"So you wanted to become an ex-virgin," I said to him as I wiped my hands on a napkin and stuffed my trash into the paper bag they give you at Five Guys, like every order is a to-go order.

"Yes," he said.

His cheeks were pink, though he didn't seem ashamed of what he'd said at all. More, it was as if sharing it felt a little new just yet, which made him seem shy. Which made me want to lay my non-existent cloak at his feet, and bid him to give me his hand so I might guide him over a treacherous path.

Boy, if I was already making poetry in my head, I was practically a goner. I'd never been a goner before, not really, so this was all new to me. I advised myself to take my time, but it was hard, when he was looking at me so sweetly.

"And that's why you showed up at The Breakers that night. Only you got cold feet. Or a cold dick," I added with a laugh, looking at him to see how he would respond to the crudeness.

While his expression was lofty and disdainful and, really, quite elegant, there was a smile at the corners of his lovely mouth and sparks of laughter in his eyes. He was pretending to be affronted, but, yeah, there was that sense of humor again.

"And you?" he asked, copying my movements as he cleaned up the trash from his side of the table, which included some of my trash, which just went to show what kind of guy he was. The kind that didn't mind helping another fellow out. "Why were you at The Breakers looking for me?"

"I wanted your number," I said, but while it was the truth, it wasn't the whole truth. And if I wanted to get closer to this guy, then I needed to make myself clear, along with being honest. "That, and I think you have a great ass. And," I pointed at him, smiling. "I like the way you blush. And know all the big words. Among other things."

The other things I didn't list were almost too personal for me to say. I'm not that guy who sends cards with hearts and flowers. I also wasn't used to saying out loud those things I often thought in the silence of my head. But maybe, with this guy, it was time.

"I like getting my dick sucked by just about anyone who will do it," I said to him, enjoying the way his eyebrows rose with shock. "But mostly—" I paused to get it together, so the words wouldn't come out in a tumble and be so incomprehensible that I'd have to say it out loud twice instead of just the once. "I like to cuddle afterwards."

"Cuddle?" he asked me, though I looked around the restaurant instead of into those blue eyes of his.

"Yeah," I said. "Now you know."

"You can look at me, you know," he said. "Look at me, Nick."

Oh, boy. With a voice like that I couldn't help but obey him and, when I did, his expression was kind.

"You're big softie, aren't you, Nick." This was not a question.

"Yeah," I said, and the single word drew itself out with such reluctance that I had to laugh at myself. "But you can't tell. Not anyone. Ever. Promise me."

"I promise," he said in that sweet way he had which belied the laughter underneath.

"Now that I've confessed," I said, getting back to business. "Can I have your number, please?"

"Yes, you may," he said, polite as anything as he reached for my phone.

When I gave it to him, I was mesmerized by the elegant way his fingers curled around the edges, and the serious expression on his face as he tapped his number in. Visions of those fingers curling around my cock as he gazed up at me with that same seriousness while giving me a blowjob almost ruined the moment. But I was able to reach down and adjust myself, shifting in my seat like I had to move because I was uncomfortable and not because I had a cock as hard as a canon.

"So maybe we can go on a real date sometime," I said as I took my phone back from him. "Maybe tomorrow night? I can make reservations for us, if you'd like." Already I was going over a list of likely restaurants in town, as small-town Harlin was surprisingly packed with great little places to take a date.

"Sure," he said, surprising me a little, and his smile was bright and brilliant like he was pleased to be asked.

"How 'bout I pick you up around seven?" I asked, inordinately pleased with myself. It was an easy victory to have him say yes to dinner at some fancy place without even going to coffee first, but maybe Five Guys had been the ice breaker I never knew I needed.

"That sounds fine," he said. "But I guess you'll need my address too."

We exchanged phones and entered all of our information into the other guy's phone like a couple of fifth graders becoming best friends. Then we had to part ways, and I thought about kissing him, and then thought about it again as we went out of Five Guys and stood on the sidewalk in the chilly air for a minute, our hands in our pockets, both of our mouths opening in round circles so we could pretend we were blowing smoke.

"Maybe you could kiss me now," he said, looking at me all serious and sweet.

"You've never been kissed," I said, knowing the answer was no, but wanting confirmation. If this was his first kiss, I wanted it to be a good one. He deserved it for waiting to long.

"No, I have not," he said.

"All right," I said, and pulled my hands out of my pockets to tug on the lapels of his thick woolen coat. When we were close enough so that the tips of my boots met the tips of his shiny shoes, I tightened my grip a little to keep him where he was and then leaned in, nice and slow, so he'd know exactly where I was and wouldn't be startled.

He closed his eyes, and I closed mine and though our noses bumped, it was gently, and though our mouths were cold they soon warmed, and I did it slow. Slow, slow, slow, silky soft, tipping my tongue on the edge of his upper lip, a caress, a bit of affection that turned into a feeling that went deeper and turned smoky and sweet. Kissing him was like being drawn underwater in arms that held and pulled me close and he wasn't even touching me, not at all.

When I pulled back I was out of breath like I'd been running or had surfaced after a long, sweet, still time. I opened my eyes. We were so close, I was looking right into his eyes, felt the snap of energy between us, and licked my lips to catch the traces of the taste of him.

"Oh, my," he said, his fingers brushing his mouth like he wanted to capture the taste of me, as well.

"See you tomorrow at seven," I said, doing my I'm-so-suave-you-can't-resist-me voice, though at that point I knew I didn't really need it. Didn't need any of my usual tricks with this guy, didn't want to use them, either. Old habits died hard, though, so I was going to give myself a pass.

"I'm looking forward to it," he said, and I could see in his eyes that he meant it.

Getting in my car and driving home, I felt like I was floating. I had a date with Daniel, and then, after, we might have sex. And then we'd cuddle, the best part. Maybe, maybe.

Chapter Five

After spending a good deal of time on Saturday with chores and laundry, in the hopes that Daniel would be willing to come back to my place after our date, I hopped in the shower and went through all the steps of getting myself ready for our date. I used more soap than was necessary, and jerked off before and after, just so I wouldn't appear too eager when I picked him up. I lathered on cologne, took half of it off, and then walked around with a towel wrapped around my waist, waving both hands at my neck to get the cologne to dissipate.

I wanted to go slow with this guy, wanted things to build between us in a slow and gracious way so they would last. And, of course, what I really wanted was for the sex to lead to massive amounts of cuddles. Maybe even a sleep-over because yes, I was a twelve-year old on the inside, always. So, with clean sheets on the bed, and brand new tighty-whities under my newest pair of jeans, feeling sexy as hell, I threw on my jacket, grabbed my phone and my keys and headed for the door at a quarter to seven.

The phone vibrated in my back pocket, so out of reflex

I grabbed it and answered it, and stood there with the door open, the keys hanging from my hand, listening to Daniel talk way too fast.

"I'm so sorry, so so sorry," he said, all in a rush. "My parents are here, and they want to talk. I have to cancel. It's such short notice, but I'm hoping that if we talk, you know? Maybe they're ready to understand."

It had only been a few weeks since they'd washed their hands of him, so I doubted anything could be fixed inside of a single visit. But his voice was full of hope, and I didn't want to be the person who stomped on his dreams, so I nodded, though there was no one to see it.

"Sure, no worries," I said, silently closing the door and turning the deadbolt. I folded the keys in my hand so he wouldn't hear them jingle. "Maybe we can go to coffee tomorrow and you can tell me about it."

I didn't know what the protocol was with this because when I came out, it'd been a whole lot of yes-and-we-love-you from my folks and from pretty much everyone I knew. Poor Daniel, though, his was a trickier situation all the way around. I wanted to help him as much as I could. I wanted him to be happy. And damn it, I wanted those cuddles.

"Yes," he said, a bit breathless, and I got the feeling he was holding the phone with both hands, for his voice sounded muffled. "I've got to go. See you at noon at the Brewing Market tomorrow?"

"You got it," I said, throwing an extra layer of every-thing-is-going-to-be-okay in there, in the hopes of being soothing. "See you."

He hung up and I hung up and then I stood there in my little entryway, looking down at my carefully chosen jeans and button-down white shirt and emerald silk tie to match my eyes. A moment ago I'd felt sexy and hopeful. Now I was a sad panda, all on his own with no prospect of a meal shared while staring into those deep blue eyes, watching him wipe that lush mouth of his with a cloth napkin.

There would be no holding hands over desert. No walking hand-in-hand to my car. Nothing romantic. Only me scrambling to come up with a way to fill the blank void that was suddenly now my evening. In the back of which was a cloud of worry about dear, sweet Daniel who only wanted that his parents should be kind to him and accept him.

Shrugging off my jacket and putting the keys and the phone on the counter, I changed into my softest t-shirt and sweats. I made a can of Spaghettios, which I keep in the cupboard for emergencies, added some chopped up hot dogs to the saucepan, and stirred it all together until it was hot and yummy.

I ate this mess while sitting on the couch and watching murder TV, feeling sorry for myself the entire while. When I was done, I went into the kitchen where I intended to rinse out the bowl and saucepan, and then dig into my freezer for whatever ice cream was hiding in there, just like a lovesick teenager.

At first I thought I was imagining the knock on my door, which sounded so tentative that I heard it the way you do when it's the walls of a building settling around you, that is, with only part of my attention. Then the knock came again, a little more rapid this time and far too loudly and insistently to be the creaking of wood and plaster. There was someone at the door.

Thinking it might be Troy for some reason, I went to the door and flung it open, standing there in my ratty sweats and t-shirt. And there stood Daniel, in a once-dapper outfit of wool trousers and a button-down white shirt and, probably, at one point, a tie. Only now the collar of the shirt was askew because he'd ripped off the tie, it seemed, and he was shivering in his wool coat. Tear-streaks stained his face, and he looked at me as though he wanted to know the secret that only I could tell him.

"What happened?" I asked, pulling him inside and shutting and locking the door. "Are you okay?"

We were so close in that little foyer of mine that he was almost stepping on my bare feet, and I could feel the heat coming off his body, though he was shaking with little tremors. I was about to wave him further in and offer him a beer from my fridge when he whipped off his coat and let it fall to the floor. The next thing I knew, he was in my arms, his arms around my neck like he was about to drown. And maybe he was.

Near as I could figure, the meeting with the parents had gone horribly wrong and, other than Troy and his aunt and uncle, I was the only person he knew in town. And maybe that was it, or maybe it was something else. I needed to find out and fast, because that would tell me what I needed to do for him.

Pulling back, I kept my arm around his shoulder, and used my thumb to trace the faint dampness beneath his sad blue eyes.

"Was it your folks?" I asked, quite gently.

"Yes," he said with a shaky nod. "On the phone they made it sound hopeful. But then we met at the restaurant, and it started even as we were waiting for our table. It got so bad, they were so angry and disappointed—I didn't stick around after I figured it out, but since they picked me up, I had to get a taxi here. Maybe our date can still be on?"

Letting out a slow breath, I shook my head as I tidied his collar and clasped his neck gently with my hands. I was astonished that he was worried about me when the roof had just caved in on the last of his dreams about having a good relationship with his parents.

"We can have our date right here," I told him. "I've got another can of Spaghettios I can heat up for you, and there's beer in the fridge, and maybe ice cream for later. Sound good?"

"Can I spend the night?" he asked.

His eyes were enormous, and his face was white. I got the feeling that part of this request might be in reaction to his parents' rejection. Maybe staying over was his way of proving to himself that coming out as gay would be worth it, or maybe staying over was because he really liked the idea of a sleepover complete with cuddles. What I couldn't do, of course, was assume that his passion for me was enough, if indeed he had any passion and this all wasn't just a knee-jerk reaction.

"Would that be on the couch?" I asked as I traced my thumb along his jawbone. "Or in my bed with me?"

"I'm a grown man," he said. "I know what I want."

The words came out rough, like defiance and anger all rolled into one. There was no way I wanted to take advantage of him, even as my whole body felt it was on alert at his nearness, at the scent of him, at the adorable way his golden hair curled behind his ears. What I did want to do was take care of him.

"I know you do," I said to him, without the least bit of judgment. "Why don't you come in and settle on the couch while I make you something to eat. Then we can go from there."

With a wave, I guided him into my apartment, got him a beer from the fridge, and handed him the remote so he could sit on the couch and channel surf while I heated up my other can of Spaghettios though, alas, I was out of hot dogs. When I handed him the bowl of food and settled on the couch beside him, he smiled at me.

"I've not had these since I was a kid," he said, shoveling in a mouthful.

I had been on the verge of saying that when he cancelled our date, I made myself feel better with comfort food. But I didn't want him to feel bad about it, seeing as he'd probably jumped at the chance of him and his parents coming to an understanding over a nice meal. Instead, I patted his thigh, took the remote, found us a nice documentary to watch, and let the sense of comfort settle around us while we learned about dinosaurs and how they'd died out after the giant meteor had hit earth.

All the while he was finishing his Spaghettios, he'd not touched his beer, though when he got up to take his bowl and spoon to the sink, I noticed that when he came back, he sat quite close. His thigh touched my thigh, and there wasn't any room for me to mistake what he had done.

It was amazing how good he smelled and how my body reacted to his nearness and how, when he leaned into me so that I had to loop an arm over his shoulder, I wasn't sorry at all.

"Were there lines drawn in the sand?" I asked him as I tipped my neck to rest my cheek on the top of his head.

"Yes, by them and then by me," he said, his voice quite low. "I can't not be who I am. Not with how far I've come." With a small shift of his body, he leaned into me, his face against my neck, his breath warm and soft on my skin. "Not with how far I want to go."

"Are you sure?" I asked.

I didn't want this to be a repeat of glory hole night at The Breakers, where it seemed like a good idea at first, but then turned into a not so good idea. I'd drive him home, then and there, if I felt the least bit of hesitation from him.

But when he tipped his head back and looked up at me, I felt all of my resistance shredding away.

The dance of blue fire in those eyes and the half-lidded way he looked at me might not have been enough to convince me he knew what he wanted, but when he shifted his whole body so he was on top of me and pressing me into the back of the couch, it was. I was convinced, both by the breadth of his shoulders, the hard bone of his hips, and the warmth of his groin as he straddled my thigh.

"Hey, now," I said, looking up at him, spanning his waist with both hands.

"You could have done anything other than what you did," he said, bending close to brush his lips to mine.

"And what's that?" I asked, not having any idea what he was on about and, being completely distracted by the shiver that ran all the way through me at the brief kiss.

"Being a gentleman every single time," he said. "I've got a weakness for that."

Being patient with Daniel had paid off but, more, he trusted. I needed to make sure he would go on trusting me, so I tugged on his shirt and made him look at me.

"We don't have to do this," I said. "We can wait. We can wait as long as you want."

"I'm quite ready," he said, dipping his head to sweep a kiss on my forehead. "All of me feels ready. And besides, you smell amazing. You *feel* amazing. So can we agree that this is okay? And is the couch big enough for it?"

There was only so much resistance I could put up and especially not in the face of that flush on his cheeks and the way he looked down at me, the way he bent to kiss me. The warmth of him as I pulled him close. The hammer of my heart in my throat, and the rapid pulse beneath his skin as I planted kisses along his neck.

When I closed my eyes, he took my hand from his waist

and planted it on the crotch of his jeans. And when I opened my eyes, I heard as well as saw him take a shuddery breath. His mouth was the color of raspberries and the flush on his cheeks was sweet and pink. All I could see in his eyes was the darkness of his pupils and the dapple of sweat on his brow.

"You should be my first," he said, almost breathless. "I want you to be. Please?"

There was no way I could resist that kind of request, all shy and bold at the same time. So I didn't. I tumbled him on the couch until he was beneath me, and felt him moving as he toed off his shoes. Then I unzipped his fly, slipping my hand between our bodies, and tugged down his underwear to take his very hard, very warm cock in my hand. His whole body twitched and his eyebrows flew up as I settled on my elbow and shifted our bodies, planting myself along the length of the couch, so I could jerk him off nice and slow.

"Stop me any time," I said, being a smartass, knowing he would not want me to, knowing he did not want me to, not with the way he was arching beneath me. There was sweat on his throat as he threw his head back, and when I pulled up my hand to lave a nice long lick along my palm, his heavy-lidded eyes tracked every move I made.

"Take a deep breath," I said, watching his chest hitch. "I'm not going to hurt you. I'll be so, so gentle with you."

As he breathed in, his chest rose and fell, and I leaned forward to kiss him and then settled in to giving him the best hand job he'd ever had. Or at least the very first one from another guy. I stroked him slow and then a little fast, tracking his responses, storing them away. I petted him and teased him and slicked him up and made it good.

I wanted it to be amazing, I wanted it to make him feel that yes, this was right, both for him and for me. His cock was hard and slick in my palm, and my whole body responded with pleasure as he came in my hand, a curl of white on his belly, in the dark hairs beneath his belly button, and on his fancy shirt, that I'd forgotten to tug out of the way.

As his shuddery breath turned into a sigh, I moved close to kiss him, and tucked his cock back in his underwear, pulling his zipper up halfway. Then I took him in my arms and settled him half on top of me, so he could doze and recover. So I could kiss his sweaty temple and lick the corner of his eyebrow to taste the salt of his sweat there.

"Yeah?" I asked. I didn't need to know that he enjoyed it, as he obviously had. What I wanted to know was whether or not he was okay so I could do everything in my power to fix it if it was not.

"Yeah," he said, turning his head to look up at me. "Is it your turn now?"

"We have time," I said.

I enjoyed the sight of him in my arms, as he was, languid and relaxed, those pink cheeks and raspberry mouth as it curved in a pleased smile.

"Since you're staying the night," I said, kissing him on the end of his nose. "I can let you in on the fact that I have a secret stash of Fruit Loops."

His mouth opened in a circle as he made a sound of pleasure. I kissed that mouth and tasted that pleasure, and smiled as I felt him smile, and knew that I had made the right decision, after all, in going out New Year's Eve.

I owed Troy, too, for being the catalyst for all of the joy that bubbled up inside of me at the thought of not only sharing my Fruit Loops with this guy, but the shower after we had another go around. And then, in the morning, there would be cuddles between the sheets. Although, the way Daniel tugged me down on top of him and wrapped his arms around my waist, the cuddles were already starting, that blissful closeness, that sweetness.

"I like Fruit Loops with ice cream," he whispered in my ear just before he traced his tongue down the length of my neck. "You got any?"

"Do I got any?" I asked in mock disdain. "Are you kidding. I have vanilla and I got chocolate, which do you want?"

"Vanilla," he said with a sigh as he gently nipped my earlobe. "I've been loyal to vanilla all of my life."

"You got it," I said, and vowed then and there to always have some on hand for him. It would be no hardship, and it would always be sweet. Just like being with him now was. I had been his first and I would do anything to be his always.

The End

More Books by Jackie North

Hello, Dear Reader!

Thank you for reading *The Glory of Love,* which I hope you enjoyed. And, if you did, you might enjoy some of my other books. They are currently on Amazon and available in KU. Happy Reading!

Best Regards,

Jackie

The Love Across Time Series (Time Travel Romance)
Heroes for Ghosts
Honey From the Lion
Wild as the West Texas Wind
Ride the Whirlwind
Hemingway's Notebook
For the Love of a Ghost

Love Across Time Sequels
Heroes Across Time - Sequel to Heroes for Ghosts

Holiday Standalones
The Christmas Knife
Hot Chocolate Kisses
The Little Matchboy

Standalone
The Duke of Hand to Heart

Box Set
Love Across Time

Connect with Jackie:

https://www.jackienorth.com/
jackie@jackienorth.com

facebook.com/jackienorthMM

twitter.com/JackieNorthMM

pinterest.com/jackienorthauthor

bookbub.com/profile/jackie-north

amazon.com/author/jackienorth

goodreads.com/Jackie_North

instagram.com/jackienorth_author

Author's Notes

I wrote The *Glory of Love* as part of a group release for New Year's Eve, 2019. It was tons of fun, and my second foray into writing something contemporary with a little more steam than my usual.

Also, I got to use my sweet little imaginary town of Harlin, Colorado. Now, every time I drive through the real town that it is based on, I can point to the bar that The Breakers is based on. "There," I can say. "There is where Nick met the love of his life!"

About the Author

Jackie North has written since grade school and spent years absorbing mainstream romances. Her dream was to write full time and put her English degree to good use.

As fate would have it, she discovered m/m romance and decided that men falling in love with other men was exactly what she wanted to write about.

Her characters are a bit flawed and broken. Some find themselves on the edge of society, and others are lost. All of them deserve a happily ever after, and she makes sure they get it!

She likes long walks on the beach, the smell of lavender and rainstorms, and enjoys sleeping in on snowy mornings.

In her heart, there is peace to be found everywhere, but since in the real world this isn't always true, Jackie writes for love.

Connect with Jackie:

https://www.jackienorth.com/
jackie@jackienorth.com

facebook.com/jackienorthMM

twitter.com/JackieNorthMM

pinterest.com/jackienorthauthor

bookbub.com/profile/jackie-north

amazon.com/author/jackienorth

goodreads.com/Jackie_North

instagram.com/jackienorth_author

www.ingramcontent.com/pod-product-compliance
Lightning Source LLC
Chambersburg PA
CBHW060955120626
46557CB00003B/1174